Dedicated to the memory of Irma Hadzimuratovic (1988–1995),
whose courage continues to inspire.
A. D.

For Ian Jack
C. R.

VIKING

Published by the Penguin Group
Penguin Books Ltd, 27 Wrights Lane, London W8 5TZ, England
Penguin Books USA Inc., 375 Hudson Street, New York, New York 10014, USA
Penguin Books Australia Ltd, Ringwood, Victoria, Australia
Penguin Books Canada Ltd, 10 Alcorn Avenue, Toronto, Ontario, Canada M4V 3B2
Penguin Books (NZ) Ltd, 182–190 Wairau Road, Auckland 10, New Zealand

Penguin Books Ltd, Registered Offices: Harmondsworth, Middlesex, England

First published 1996
1 3 5 7 9 10 8 6 4 2

Text copyright © Alan Durant, 1996
Illustrations copyright © Chris Riddell, 1996

The moral right of the author and illustrator has been asserted

Manufactured in China by Imago

A CIP catalogue record for this book is available from the British Library

ISBN 0-670-86924-4

Angus Rides the Goods Train

ALAN DURANT

ILLUSTRATED BY CHRIS RIDDELL

VIKING

That night Angus rode the goods train.

He awoke to the sound of clunking and chinking.

And there it was.

"All aboard!" called the driver – and Angus climbed up on to the train.

He saw milk and honey and rice and a huge tank of water to make steam for the train.

"Where are we going?" he asked

"Somewhere very important," said the driver. "Far away. Far, far away."

And with a whistle and a whoosh they were off.

Away they sped across the land and over the sea, in and out of towns and cities, up and down hills and mountains, through fields and valleys and forests thick and lush with trees . . .

The wind swept through Angus's hair and his heart was happy to be going far, far away to somewhere so important.

Then the landscape changed.

They came to a thin forest of
stunted and withered trees.

"Help us. Help us, please,"
groaned the trees. "We need water."

Angus's heart went out to the trees.
"Oh, let's stop and help them,"
he said. "We have lots of water."

But the driver would not stop.
"We have no water to spare,"
he said. "We have far to go."

And on they sped once more . . .

. . . Until they came to a place where there were lots of cages.

In each of them was a bear. The bears shook their heads and they pawed at the bars.

"We are going mad," they wailed. "We are starving."

Angus's heart went out to the bears. "Stop!" he cried. "We must stop and help. We have honey."

But the driver would not stop. "We have no honey to spare," he said.

And on they raced into the darkness . . .

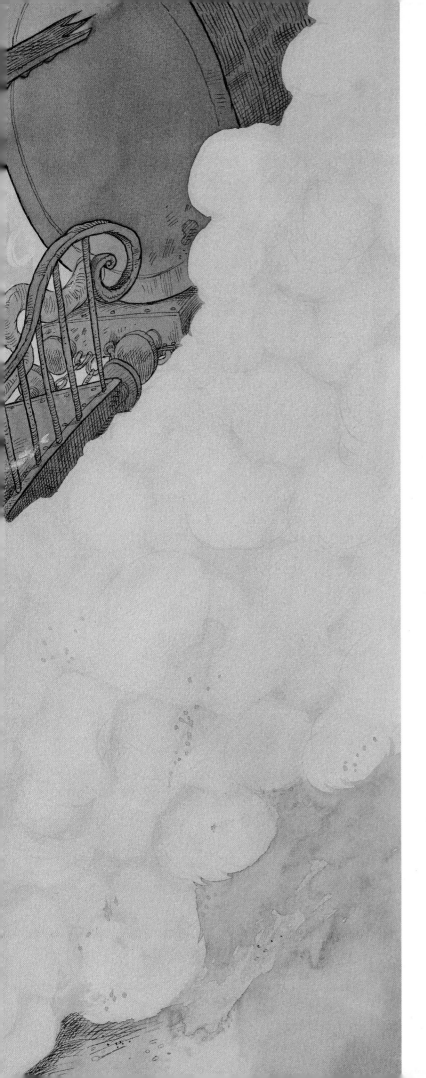

. . . Away from the towns and the woods and the fields, away from the rivers and the trees and the grass, headlong into the desert they rushed.

And there by a dune sat a mother and her crying baby.

"Help us, please," moaned the mother. "I have no milk for my baby."

Angus's heart went out to the mother and her baby. "Yes," he said, "I will help. I can give you milk."

But the driver would not stop.

Now they came to a terrible place, where the houses were all broken and the fields were full of holes. By the track stood a girl.

"Oh, please, can you help me?" she called. "I have lost my mother and my father. And I am so hungry."

Angus's heart went out to the girl. "Stop!" he cried. "Driver, please stop. We have rice to give."

But the driver drove on.

At last, as dawn broke, they arrived in a beautiful green valley.

The driver slowed down and said, "There, these are the people who our goods are for: the king and his courtiers. Every day, I bring milk and honey and rice for their breakfast."

"But there are so few of them for so much food," said Angus.

"They are very important," said the driver.

Then he put on the brake and stopped the train beside the table. He bowed very low.

"Breakfast, Your Majesty!" he said, but . . .

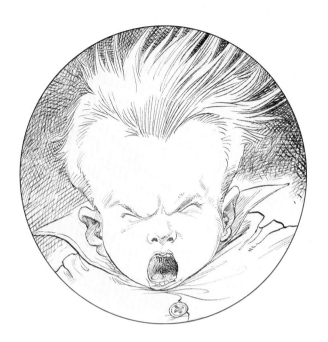

. . . "No!" cried Angus. "No, no, this is not right!" And he pushed the driver down from the train.

Angus pulled on the lever and the wheels started to turn, and he drove the goods train away from the table, away from the king and the courtiers waiting to eat, away from the driver, out of the dawn and back into the dark . . .

He came to the terrible place,
where the girl still stood.

"Climb aboard," said Angus,
"and have some rice."

On into the desert they rode, and Angus gave milk to the mother and her baby.

Angus gave honey to the caged bears.

Angus poured water on the roots of the withering trees.

When Angus arrived home to his bed, the goods train was empty and Angus was full of joy.

At breakfast, on the television, Angus saw a picture of his friend, and he watched as a man explained why they could not help, could not give, could not save.

"One day," vowed Angus, "I will drive the goods train."